lauren child

I am NOT sleepy and I WILL NOT go to bed

featuring **Charlie** and **Lola**

ORCHARD BOOKS

Perry

A special thank you to Mrs Fish at Big Fish
and hello to Little Fish

For Perry with a
squillion thanks for a
zillion favours

(p.s. i hope this typeface isn't a style crime)

For the supremely stylish,
and fantastically fabulous,

Sandro and Piera
with love from
Lauren

ORCHARD BOOKS 338 Euston Road, London NW1 3BH
Orchard Books Australia Hachette Children's Books, Level 17/205 Kent Street, Sydney NSW 2000
ISBN 1 84121 821 9 (hb)   ISBN 1 84121 078 1 (pb)
First published in Great Britain in 2001.   First paperback publication in 2002.
Text and illustrations © Lauren Child 2001
The right of Lauren Child to be identified as the author and the illustrator of this work
has been asserted by her in accordance with the Copyrights, Designs and Patents Act, 1988.
A CIP catalogue record of this book is available from the British Library
(hb) 10 9 8 7 6 5 4 3   (pb) 20 19 18 17 16
Printed in Singapore

I have this little sister Lola.
She is small and very funny.
Sometimes I have to keep an eye on her.
Sometimes Mum and Dad ask me to try and
get her off to bed.
This is a hard job
because Lola likes to stay up late.

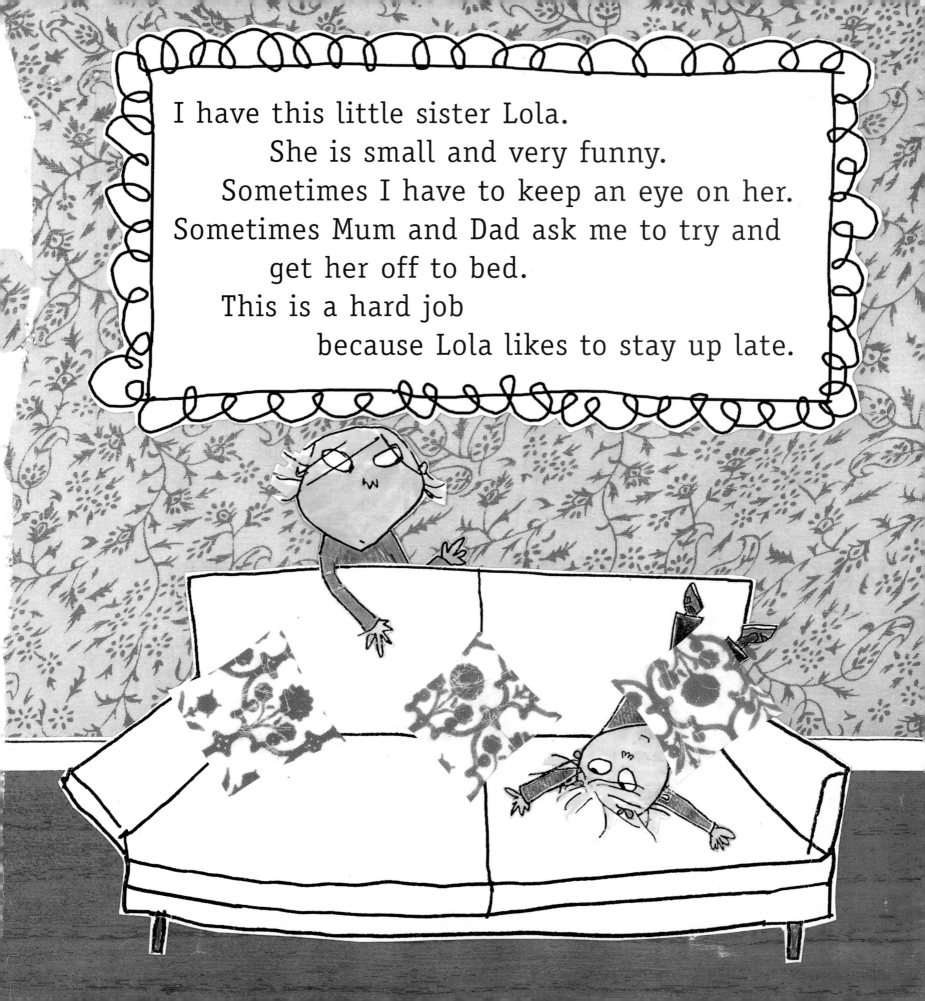

Lola likes to stay up colouring

and

scribbling

and

sticking

and

wriggling

and

bouncing

and most of all

chattering.

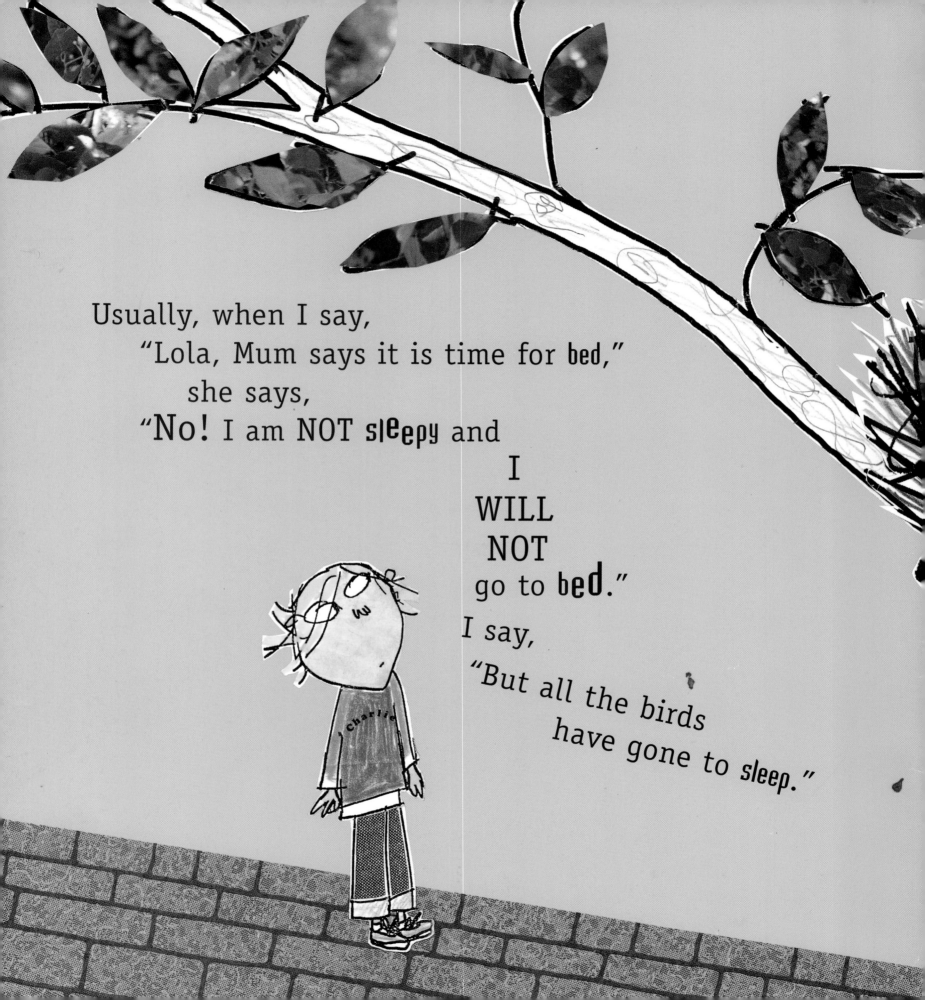

Usually, when I say,
"Lola, Mum says it is time for bed,"
she says,
"No! I am NOT sleepy and

I
WILL
NOT
go to bed."
I say,
"But all the birds
have gone to sleep."

She says,
    "But I am **not** a bird,
        Charlie."

"But you must be slightly sleepy, Lola,"
I say.

Lola says,
"I am not slightly sleepy at 6

or 7

or 8

and I am still
wide awake at 9

and not at all tired at 10

11

12

and I will probably still be perky at even **13** O'CLOCK in the morning."

Lola says she **never** gets tired.

One night I said, "But if there's no bedtime there can be no bedtime drink and it's pink milk tonight." (Lola really likes pink milk.) "Are you sure you don't want to go to bed?"

"But Charlie," says Lola, "if I have pink milk,
the tigers will want pink milk too."
"Tigers," I say, "what tigers?"
                    "The tigers at the table, Charlie,
they are waiting for their bedtime drink.
    Tigers get very cross if they have to wait."

So I make Lola and

three tigers pink milk.

Then I say,
"Let's go and brush our teeth."

So Lola says, "But Charlie, I can't brush my teeth
      because somebody is eating my toothbrush."
  "But who would eat your toothbrush?" I say.
Lola says, "I think it's that lion,
   I saw him brushing his teeth with my toothbrush
and now he's gobbling it all up."
   "But this looks like your brush, Lola," I say.
       "Oh," says Lola,
    "he must be using yours."

brush their teeth.

Then I say, "You have to have
a bath. You look a bit grubby."
"Who says?" says Lola.
"Mum does," I say. "She's coming
to check in **one** minute."
And then what do you think Lola says?
"But Charlie, I can't have a bath
because of the whales."
"What whales?
Where?"
I say,
looking
about.

Bubble Cat

Bubble Bath

"The whales who are swimming
in the bath, they're taking up all of
the room," she says.
"Well what do you want me
to do about it?" I ask.
"Maybe you will have to help me
shoo one of them down
the plug hole," says Lola.
So I help Lola shoo
one
whale
down
the
plug
hole.

And

then

Lola

hops

into

the

bath.

"Now, Lola," I say. "Where are your pyjamas?"
"I don't have any pyjamas, Charlie," she says.
I say, "What about these ones under your pillow?"
"Those are not my pyjamas," says Lola, shaking her head.
"Oh no, those pyjamas belong to
two dancing dogs."
"Well, do you think they
would let you just borrow
their pyjamas?" I ask.

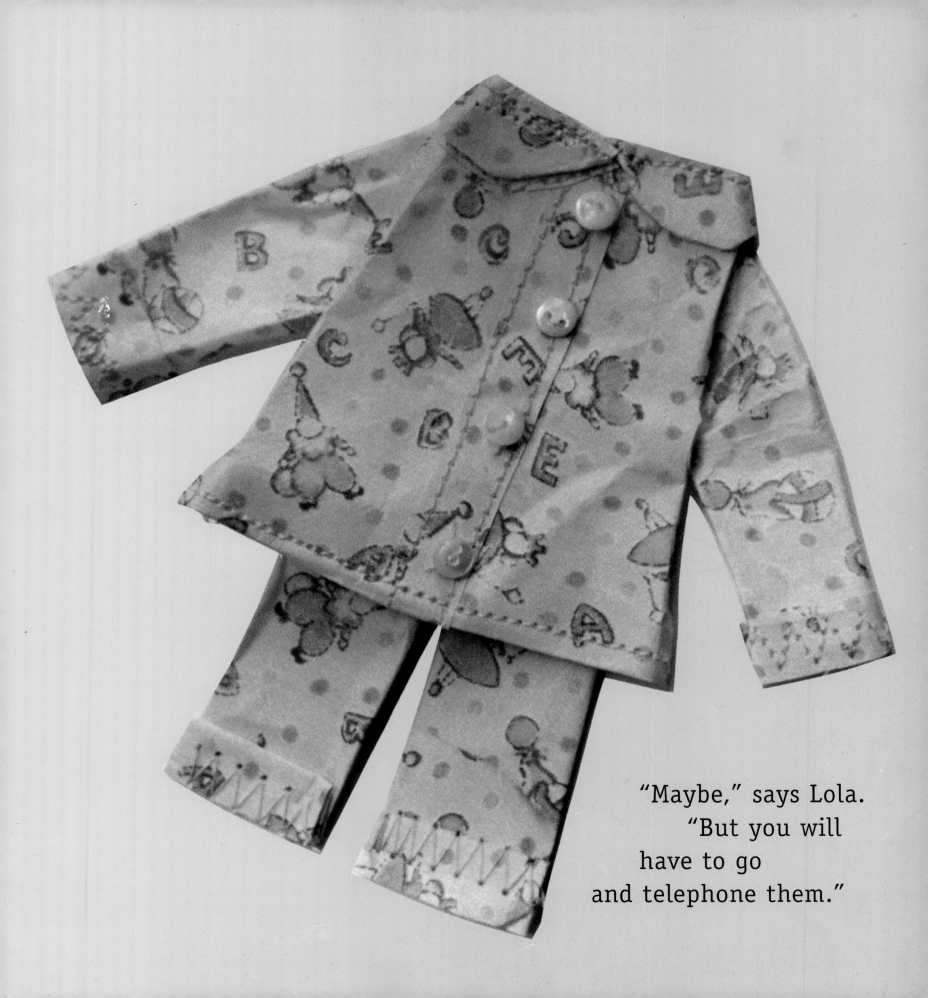

"Maybe," says Lola.
"But you will
have to go
and telephone them."

And off I go to telephone the two dancing dogs. - - -

"They say pyjamas suit you better than them.
You can wear them whenever you like." - - - - - - - - -

"What are they saying?" Lola asks.

"That's nice of them," she says.

And so Lola
pops on
her pyjamas.

At last
Lola is ready for **bed** and I say,

"Now, Lola,
I have given three **tigers**
their bedtime drink

and

watched a **lion**
gobbling my toothbrush

and

shooed one
whale
down
the
plug
hole

and

telephoned two
dancing dogs
about pyjamas.

NOW

will

you

please

hop

into

bed."

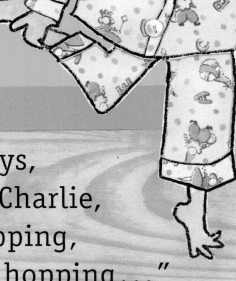

Lola says,
"Yes, yes, Charlie,
I'm hopping,
I'm hopping..."

"But I think there's one in **yours**," says Lola,
as she climbs into **bed**.

"Goodnight Charlie.
Goodnight Hipp**i**pot**i**mus."